W9-BGN-445

The Big Banana Hunt

by Patricia M. Stockland
illustrated by Ryan Haugen

visit us at
www.abdopublishing.com

Published by Magic Wagon, a division of the ABDO Publishing Group, 8000 West 78th Street, Edina, Minnesota, 55439. Copyright © 2008 by Abdo Consulting Group, Inc. International copyrights reserved in all countries. All rights reserved. No part of this book may be reproduced in any form without written permission from the publisher.
Looking Glass Library™ is a trademark and logo of Magic Wagon.

Printed in the United States.

Text by Patricia M. Stockland
Illustrations by Ryan Haugen
Edited by Nadia Higgins
Interior layout and design by Becky Daum
Cover design by Becky Daum

Library of Congress Cataloging-in-Publication Data
Stockland, Patricia M.
The big banana hunt / Patricia M. Stockland ; illustrated by Ryan Haugen.
p. cm. — (Safari friends—Milo & Eddie)
ISBN 978-1-60270-083-3
[1. Elephants—Fiction. 2. Monkeys—Fiction. 3. Bananas—Fiction. 4. Grasslands—Fiction. 5. Africa—Fiction.] I. Haugen, Ryan, 1972- ill. II. Title.
PZ7.S865Big 2008
[E]—dc22

2007036995

Milo the monkey squirmed and turned in his sleep. Suddenly, he held out his arms and shook his hands like imaginary pom-poms. Then he started cheering,

"Bananas! Bananas! Go, go bananas!
Bananas make good breakfast. Bananas make good pie!
Get me some bananas, or else I'm gonna cry!"

“Milo? Milo! Wake up!” Eddie the elephant shook his little friend awake.

“Wha—? What happened? Where am I?” Milo rubbed his eyes and patted his tummy with his tail. “Do you smell bananas?”

“You were dreaming about bananas again,” answered Eddie. “Or perhaps about a banana bake-off.”

“Oh, yes. I remember now,” Milo said. “I’m *so* hungry, Eddie. I really, really need some bananas.”

Milo opened the banana cupboard. “See?” he groaned. “Still empty!”

"Well, there's only one way I know to find bananas," Eddie suggested. "And that's to go on a big banana hunt."

"A big banana hunt? I'm a monkey, and even I have never been on one of those," said Milo.

Eddie wasn't listening. He was already packing his trunk, putting on his safari hat, and folding his maps.

"Do I need a trunk, too?" asked Milo.

"No, you just need your nose," Eddie answered.

Soon, the pair was plodding and leaping through the great, great grassland. According to Eddie's map, the first place to investigate was the Water Buffalo Bakery.

Milo scratched his head. "This doesn't seem right, Eddie."

"No, no, no. According to my map, the bakery has bananas," Eddie insisted, walking up to the counter.

"Good morning and a pleasure to be at your service," said Wally the water buffalo. "What delectable dish might I bring you this fine day?"

Eddie cleared his throat. “We would like one large bunch of bananas, if you please.”

“Bananas? . . . Are *you* bananas?” asked Wally. “This is a *bakery*, not a banana factory.” Wally spun dishes across the counter at Eddie and Milo. “But perhaps you would like to try a dung beetle doughnut? Oh, oh, I know! A mango mud pie! Do try a mango mud pie!”

Milo wrinkled his nose. Mango mud pie didn’t smell like bananas—and the dung beetle doughnut certainly didn’t either. “We really should be going, but thank you anyway,” he said, as Eddie backed away.

THE WATER BUFFALO
BAKERY
Fresh
TERMITE BREAD

MAP

As Milo and Eddie wandered down the trail, Milo thought about something Wally had said.

"Eddie, do you think bananas are made in a factory? I mean, should we be hunting for a banana factory?" Milo asked.

Eddie stopped to spread out his map on a termite mound. "I don't think I see any banana factories on here. But, wait! Here's something! We'll surely find bananas here."

Before Milo could ask where "here" was, Eddie was digging his way through mounds of dusty dirt.

Pfffft. Yech! A cloud of dust floated right into Milo's eyes and mouth.

"Just what do you think you're doing?!" a voice shouted from inside the dust cloud.

Milo peered through the cloud. Milo realized his friend was digging through the meerkats' home! "Oh, sorry," he said.

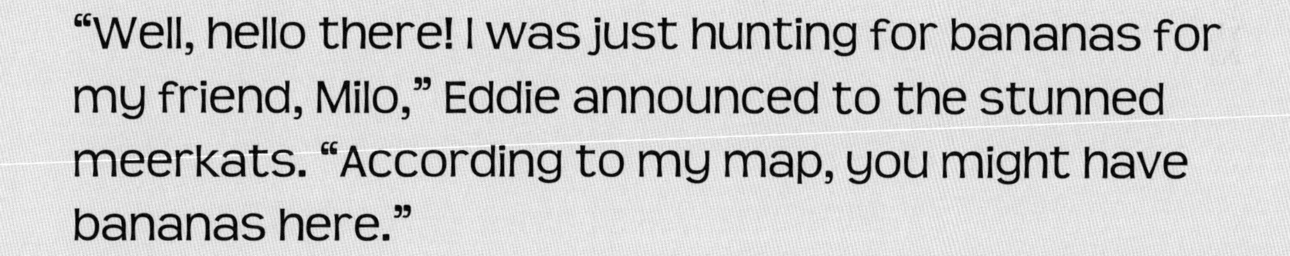

“Well, hello there! I was just hunting for bananas for my friend, Milo,” Eddie announced to the stunned meerkats. “According to my map, you might have bananas here.”

Eddie spread his map out to show everyone.

“Bananas don’t grow underground!” exclaimed the mama meerkat. “I am happy that you are willing to help your friend, but we cannot be bothered like this!”

“Wait, Mama, wait! Would Milo like to try some of our lunch? It is really, really yummy.” The baby meerkat offered a plate to Milo.

Milo looked at the plate. It did *not* smell like bananas, but he tried to be polite anyway. “Um, excuse me, but would you mind telling me what this is—exactly?” Milo asked.

“Delicious cinnamon centipede, of course!” the baby meerkat said. “Mmmmmm,” the other meerkats joined in.

Eddie cringed at the creepy crawler on the plate. “Um, we really should be going,” he said. “So sorry about the mess! Bye-bye!”

“Milo,” said Eddie as the pair moved on, “I think my map is wrong. Maybe there aren’t any bananas around here.”

Milo was stumped. How could this be? A savanna with no bananas? As he and Eddie turned toward home, his little tummy started to grumble and rumble. It even made a hiccup sound.

Milo was so worried about his tummy, and Eddie was so worried about his misguided map, that the two weren't even watching the trail when—*thwack!*

"Oooow! What in the great, great grasslands was *that?*" Eddie sat, rubbing his head with his trunk. The two had walked straight into a tree.

Milo sniffed. "*Bananas!* I smell *bananas!*" The monkey scrambled up the tree trunk.

"Milo? Where'd you go?" The monkey had disappeared so quickly that Eddie hadn't even see him climb the tree.

"It's a banana bonanza!" Milo yelled from a branch. He did a little tap dance. As he plucked bananas, he sang, "One banana, two banana, three banana, four . . ."

Bonk! As Eddie looked up, a bulky bunch of bananas fell beside him.

"Milo! You found bananas!" Eddie cheered.

"Five banana, six banana," Milo continued, "who could ask for anything more?"

Bonk. Bonkety-boing. Splat! Soon, it was raining bananas everywhere!

Milo stayed up in the tree and ate bananas for a long time. Then, something amazing happened: the monkey got full. His belly and cheeks stuffed with bananas, Milo climbed down.

"Eddie! Can you believe it?" Milo said, picking up bananas from the ground. "Bananas grow on trees! I'm rich!"

"Well, actually," said Eddie, "according to my field guide, this 'tree' is a type of herb plant and not really a tree. You can plant the herbs yourself, and if you mix the potting dirt with cocoa powder, you can grow chocolate-covered bananas!"

"Oh, Eddie," Milo sighed, "I don't know if I trust your field guides anymore. You may want to go to the library and get some better books. But would you care to try one of my bananas?"

"Why, thank you very much!" Eddie smiled.

"Not at all," replied Milo. "You know, bananas also make a great pie. In fact, that reminds me of beautiful song."

Bananas in hand, Milo the monkey and Eddie the elephant made their way home. All the while, the monkey sang to his friend,

"Bananas! Bananas! Go, go, bananas!
Bananas make good breakfast. Bananas make good pie!
You're my banana buddy, fiddely-do, diddely-dum, fiddely-die!"

Savanna Facts

Only a few types of monkeys remain on the African savanna. These include patas monkeys, vervet monkeys, and some baboons. Many other types of monkeys are found in the tropical forests of Africa.

Patas monkeys are omnivores. This means they eat fruits and vegetables as well as meat.

Bananas don't have to be yellow. Some ripen to red or purple.

Plantains are a type of banana that are picked green. Plantains can also ripen to yellow. They can be cooked, stewed, fried, or dried.